A Step into History

I Have a Dream

The Life of Martin Luther King, Jr.

by
Eric Metzgar

Don Johnston Incorporated
Volo, Illinois

2

Edited by:

Jerry Stemach, MS, CCC-SLP

Gail Portnuff Venable, MS, CCC-SLP

Dorothy Tyack, MA

Consultant:

Ted S. Hasselbring, PhD

Graphics and Illustrations:

Photographs and illustrations are all created professionally
and modified to provide the best possible support for the
intended reader.

Pages 5: Library of Congress, Prints & Photographs Division,
[HABS GA,61-ATLA,48-11]

Page 11: Library of Congress, Prints & Photographs Division,
[LC-DIG-ppmsca-05629]

Page 28: © Kanu Gandhi/Gandhiserve

Pages 31, 58, 63, 76, 79, 84: © AP/Wide World Photos

Pages 38, 50, 60, 69, and front cover: © Bettmann/CORBIS

All other photos © Don Johnston Incorporated and its licensors.

Narration:

Professional actors and actresses read the text to build
excitement and to model research-based elements of fluency:
intonation, stress, prosody, phrase groupings and rate.

The rate has been set to maximize comprehension for the reader.

Published by:

Don Johnston Incorporated
26799 West Commerce Drive
Volo, IL 60073

800.999.4660 USA Canada
800.889.5242 Technical Support
www.donjohnston.com

DON JOHNSTON

International Standard Book Number
ISBN-10: 1-4105-0621-5
ISBN-13: 978-1-4105-0621-4

Contents

Chapter 1
The Lesson of Love **5**

Chapter 2
"You Can't Sit There" **14**

Chapter 3
Love and Hate **22**

Chapter 4
New Beginnings **31**

Chapter 5
Rosa Parks **38**

Chapter 6
Proud to Walk **44**

Chapter 7
No More Segregation **52**

Chapter 8
March On! **60**

Chapter 9
I Have a Dream **69**

Chapter 10
The Last Day **79**

Bibliography **87**
About the Author **89**
About the Narrator **91**

Chapter 1

The Lesson of Love

This is the house where Martin Luther King, Jr., grew up.

One afternoon in 1935, my best friend said, "My dad says that I can't be friends with you any more." I was shocked. I was only six years old, and I couldn't understand it. I ran home crying and burst through the front door of my family's house in Atlanta, Georgia.

My parents heard me crying, and they ran downstairs. I told them what had happened. I had never seen them so sad. They wiped my tears away and sat me down. Then they tried to explain why it was not easy to be a black person in the South.

My parents told me that my best friend could no longer play with me because he was white and I was black.

"But he's my friend!" I cried.

My mother answered, "We'll try to explain that to you, Martin. But this will be difficult to hear."

"But why?" I asked.

"It's a long story," said my father. "You see, son, for many years white people *owned* black people. This was called slavery."

"Black people were kidnapped from their homes in Africa and they were brought to the United States to work as slaves on farms in the South," my mother added.

"White slave owners often beat their slaves and treated them like animals," said my father.

I could hardly believe my ears, but my parents had never lied to me, so I knew it must be true.

"Slavery lasted for over 250 years," said my mother.

"And then in the 1860s, this country was torn apart by the Civil War," my mother went on. "The war was mostly about slavery. And when the war was over, President Abraham Lincoln finally gave an order that helped to end slavery in America."

"But even though slavery is gone now, life for black people is still hard," said my father. "Even now, in 1935. Even today, most white people in the South don't want us to have the same rights as whites."

"What do you mean?" I asked.

"Well, we can't get the same jobs as white people, and we can't go to the same schools. And in a lot of places, black people can't even vote. Black people can't eat in the same restaurants as white people. We can't watch movies in the same movie theaters as white people," said my father.

"We can't even drink from the same water fountains as white people," my mother explained.

A drinking fountain with a sign showing that it was for black people only

"But why? Why don't white people like us?" I asked.

My mother took a deep breath as she tried to find the right words. Finally, she said, "Martin, this is hard to explain. All I can say is that some folks don't have enough love in their hearts."

My father nodded and said, "Some white folks will never like you — just because your skin is dark. It's called racism, son. Racism means that people from one race hate people from another race."

"Well then, I'm going to hate all white people!" I said.

"No, Martin," my father said gently. "We must love everyone, even if they don't show love towards us. This will be a hard lesson to learn, but you must try."

I thought my parents were probably right about this, but I was still angry and confused. I went to bed, but I couldn't sleep. I lay there for hours, staring at the ceiling. And from then on, I never looked at the world in the same way again.

Chapter 2

"You Can't Sit There"

It turned out that my parents were right. Being a black person was not easy, especially in the South, where we lived.

Over the next few years, I learned for myself how black people were kept apart from white people. This was called segregation.

I still remember a day when my father took me shopping for shoes in a store downtown. We sat in some empty seats at the front of the store.

A young white man came up to us and said, "I'll be happy to wait on you if you'll just move to those seats in the back." He was really telling us that black people were not allowed to sit in the seats at the front of the store.

I stood up to move, but my dad grabbed my hand and sat me down again. My dad sat up straight and proud and said, "There's nothing wrong with these seats. We'll be just fine here."

"Sorry," said the white shoe salesman, "but you *have* to move."

"Either we sit here, or we don't buy shoes at all," said my father in an angry voice.

The shoe salesman walked away. My father took my hand and walked me out of the store. I had never seen my dad so angry.

As we walked back to the car, my father said to me, "I don't care how long I have to live with segregation, I will never accept it."

A few years later, when I was 14, I was chosen to be in a public speaking contest in Dublin, Georgia. I went there on the bus with one of my teachers. The town was about 90 miles from my home.

When it was my turn to give a speech at the contest, I spoke about black people and segregation. I was nervous, but my voice was strong. After the other students had given their speeches, the judge announced the winner.

"There were many good speeches," the judge said. "But the winner today is Martin Luther King, Jr." I could not believe it! I had won the contest.

That night, my teacher and I were riding the bus back to our town. The bus was crowded and, along the way, some white people got on. The bus driver turned to my teacher and me and said, "Get up, you two. You're going to have to give up your seats."

I didn't move, so the bus driver — a white man — began to curse at me.

My teacher said to me, "Martin, we don't want any trouble. We should obey the law."

So we got up and let the white people sit down. We had to stand up all the way home for an hour and a half!

I will never forget that day. One minute I was proud and happy, and the next minute I was as angry as I had ever been in my life.

Chapter 3

Love and Hate

I left high school early and went to Morehouse College in Atlanta, Georgia, when I was only 15 years old. By the time I was 19, I had my college degree, and I had also become a Baptist minister like my father. I could have become a preacher in my father's church right after college, but I knew I still had a lot to learn. So I kept going to school for another eight years! Morehouse was in the South, but I spent most of the next eight years in the North.

In 1951, I went to study at Boston University in Boston, Massachusetts. I had always heard that black people were treated better in the North than in the South, but I learned that racism was a problem in the North as well.

I remember trying to find a place to live near the school. I went into one place after another — every place where I saw a room for rent sign. But when the landlords saw that I was black, they would always say that the room had already been rented. *Oh, sure*, I thought.

I tried not to get discouraged by the racism all around me. I studied as hard as I could. I made many friends and I tried to love everyone, just like my parents had taught me. I even made a few white friends. They treated me very well, and I learned that not all white people were racists.

I spent a lot of time thinking about the problem of racism. I thought about the struggles that black people like myself had faced over the years.

We should be treated just like everyone else, I thought.

We should be allowed to do everything that white people are allowed to do. We should have the same rights as anyone else. We didn't have those rights. I felt like a bird trapped in a cage. I wanted to bring an end to segregation, but I didn't know where to begin. The problem was so big, and I was just one person.

Then one day, I went to a class to learn about a man from India named Mahatma Gandhi. I had heard great things about him, and I wanted to learn more.

I learned that during Gandhi's time, England had ruled India, but the people of India wanted to rule themselves. Gandhi became their leader in their fight for freedom. But Gandhi didn't fight with guns — he used words of love and peace instead. He got the people of India to stop following the laws that England had made, and slowly he won freedom for his country. I was so interested in Gandhi's peaceful ways that I went to the bookstore after class, and I bought ten books about Gandhi. Then I went home and read them all.

Mahatma Gandhi used words of love and peace to fight for the freedom of his people in India.

The books made me think about love and hate in a simple way.

Hate is like a disease, I thought. *It can spread from one person to the next, and it has the power to infect everyone. But love is like medicine. It can heal a person's soul. Love has the power to bring people together.*

If I hate my enemies, they will always be my enemies, I thought. *But if I love my enemies, maybe one day they will become my friends.*

I kept thinking about racism, hate, and love. I knew that one day I would put my thoughts into action.

Chapter 4

New Beginnings

Martin Luther King, Jr. and his wife Coretta Scott King

In 1953, I married a wonderful woman named Coretta Scott. We wanted to raise a family, so I needed to find a job. We were living in Boston at the time.

In 1954, I was offered a job as a preacher in a church in Montgomery, Alabama. Alabama is a southern state and black people in Alabama were treated very poorly there. Things were better in the North where we were living.

I said to Coretta, "I'm excited about this job. I know that preachers can make a difference in peoples' lives, and I want to help people in every way I can. But I'm also afraid to live in Alabama. There's a lot of racism and segregation down there, and I don't know if we should raise our children in a place like that."

We talked and talked about living in Alabama. We talked about our fears. Neither of us wanted our children growing up with segregation and racism. We wanted our children to feel loved.

We wanted our children to feel that they were as important as anyone else.

Finally, I said to Coretta, "I don't know what to do."

My wife was brave. She said, "Martin, we were raised in the South. We must not hide from segregation. We must be strong. We must fight for the rights of black people in the places where they need us the most."

I thought about Coretta's words, and I decided that she was right.

We could not let our fears control our future.

"You're right," I said. "If we run from segregation, things will never change."

So I accepted the preaching job, and we moved from Boston to Montgomery.

We moved into a black neighborhood and made many friends. We had our first child, a little girl, and we named her Yolanda.

I continued my studies of religion, and in June 1955, I got a Ph.D. degree and became *Dr*. Martin Luther King. I spent most of my time at the church. I prayed with people and talked to them about their troubles.

During that time, many black people came to me and said, "We are tired of being treated unfairly. It's time for black people to be treated as equals."

I listened carefully to their concerns. "I understand," I told them. "Be patient a little while longer. Someday soon, things are going to change."

Chapter 5

Rosa Parks

Rosa Parks sitting at the front of a bus in Montgomery, Alabama

One day in 1955, a black woman named Rosa Parks got on a bus in Montgomery. She saw an empty seat near the front of the bus and sat down. She knew the rule that blacks had to sit in the back of the bus, so she wasn't surprised when the bus driver told her to get up and give her seat to a white man. But Rosa refused to get up, so the bus driver called the police. The police came and arrested Rosa and took her to jail.

A friend of mine called me and told me the story. His voice was angry as he spoke.

"Black people have taken this kind of treatment for too long!" my friend said.

I told him I agreed with him. "What do you think we should do?" I asked.

"It's time for a boycott! I say we boycott the buses. I say we stop riding the buses until we can sit where we want! We have to let white people know that we will not give up until we end segregation!" my friend said.

I thought a bus boycott was a great idea, but I knew that we would need the support of all the black people in Montgomery to make it work. So we put signs up in the black neighborhoods. The signs said, "On Monday, do not ride the bus to work, to town, to school, or anyplace."

That night I prayed to God. I closed my eyes and said, "Dear Lord, please make me strong. Please make my black brothers and sisters strong."

I kept praying, "The time has come for us to stand up for our rights. Give us courage. Let tomorrow be the first day of great change. Let us begin this great change with love in our hearts," I said to God.

I could hardly sleep on Sunday night because our boycott was going to begin the next morning. I walked back and forth in my bedroom while Coretta tried to calm me down. "Just be strong, my dear," she said. "This is only the beginning."

Chapter 6

Proud to Walk

I didn't get much sleep that night. Coretta and I woke up very early on Monday morning. There was a bus stop right in front of our house, so Coretta and I stood out there and waited for a bus to come. We would soon see if there were any black people on the bus. When no bus came, I decided to go back inside and make breakfast.

That's when I heard Coretta yelling, "Martin! Come quick! It's empty! The bus is empty!"

I ran to the front porch. The bus wasn't empty, but there were no black people on it! Not even one black person! Only white passengers. Coretta and I were overjoyed. The boycott was working!

But would there be black people on the next bus? We waited. Another bus came. No blacks! The black people of Montgomery had taken a first step towards equal rights. We were saying "No!" to segregation.

I drove to work that morning and, on the way, I saw a beautiful sight. The sidewalks were filled with black people *walking* to work. The most wonderful thing was that they were walking with pride in their steps!

I leaned out the window and waved and cheered at everyone. I asked one black man, "How far do you have to walk, my friend?" He smiled and yelled back, "12 miles! And I'm going to walk the whole way!" My eyes were suddenly filled with tears of joy.

I saw an old black woman crossing the street. A car pulled up beside her, and a friendly black man leaned out the window and said to her, "Jump in, Grandmother! You don't need to walk!" But the old woman just smiled and said in a proud voice, "I'm not walking for *me*. I'm walking for my children and grandchildren!" And she waved the car past her.

The white people of Montgomery had always had control over us.

But now we were standing up for ourselves, and it made the white people furious. We were glad that they were upset. At last, we had made our point. White people were finally paying attention to what black people had to say.

The white people tried everything to get us back on those buses. They would throw us in jail for almost no reason at all. They would call us on the phone and tell us they were going to kill us. A few whites even bombed our homes.

Martin Luther King, Jr. being taken to jail by a police officer

The black people in my town were scared. As their preacher, they looked to me to give them strength, so at night, at my church, I gave speeches to encourage them. I told them to stay off the buses. I told them to be brave. I told them that God would bless us with good fortune.

Chapter 7

No More Segregation

We stayed off the buses for one whole year. Some of us walked to work in the rain and snow. Some of us set up carpools.

It was a long year. Sometimes it seemed like we had not made any progress at all. Sometimes we even wondered if it had all been a big mistake, because after a year, there was still segregation in Montgomery.

Then on December 21, 1956, we got great news.

Rosa Parks had been put on trial and her case had gone all the way to the Supreme Court of the United States. The Supreme Court is the highest court in the land, and the judges had decided that segregation on buses was illegal!

We were so happy! All of our hard work had paid off. We felt a new sense of pride. It was truly an important moment in American history.

Early the next morning, I sat on my front porch waiting for the bus to come.

There were many television and
newspaper reporters standing in my
front yard. For the first time, black
people would sit beside white people on
a bus in the South!

At 5:45, a bus arrived. The door
opened, and the bus driver smiled at
me and asked, "Are you Martin Luther
King, Jr.?"

"Yes, I am," I answered.

"We're glad to have you this
morning," he said.

I smiled and thanked the bus driver and I took a seat right up front. The bus drove away as the newspaper reporters took pictures.

Down the road, white people got on the bus. Some of them did not seem to mind that I was sitting up front. But other white people were furious.

"I would rather die than sit behind a nigger!" said one white man. White slave owners used to call their slaves "nigger," and it was a very rude and insulting thing to say.

But even though I was insulted by that word, I just sat up straight in my seat and smiled.

As I rode the bus to church that morning, I thought about the progress we had made. I thought about Gandhi's peaceful ways and the advice that my parents had given me. I remembered the time that my teacher and I had to stand up on the bus for an hour and a half.

I was joyful and I was thankful. We had won our first battle.

Martin Luther King, Jr. takes his first bus ride after segregation on the buses was ended. King is the man in the hat sitting by the window.

And instead of using our hands to fight, we had used our hearts and minds. I hoped that our bus boycott would set an example across America. I knew that black people still had many struggles ahead, but winning this victory gave me hope.

Chapter 8

March On!

Martin Luther King, Jr. and his wife Coretta lead a march for civil rights, from the city of Selma to the city of Montgomery, Alabama.

We did not just sit back and enjoy our victory. Instead, we set higher goals for ourselves. In 1957, I became president of a group called the SCLC. That stands for Southern Christian Leadership Conference. We planned to work on getting rid of segregation all across the South. We wanted equal rights for voting, for jobs, and for pay.

Over the next years, we did everything we could to show all of America what we wanted.

We marched in town after town and spoke out against segregation. We set up boycotts against stores and restaurants.

Many times we were thrown in jail for protesting and marching. During our marches, some white people took our side, but many white people shouted at us and called us names. People threw bricks at us and hit us with clubs. Sometimes the police used dogs to attack us. Sometimes the police sprayed us with water from fire hoses. But just like Gandhi, we did not fight back.

A man who is marching for his rights is attacked by a
police dog.

News reporters followed our progress, so Americans saw our marches and protests on television. The TV reports were important because people all over the country were upset about what they saw, and they began to tell their elected leaders to support our struggle. Then these leaders began to speak out for us.

We kept marching. Nothing could break our spirits now. By now, our fight had become known as the "civil rights movement." Everywhere we went, we sang songs about freedom.

Even when we were in jail, you could hear us singing, "We shall overcome! We shall overcome! We shall overcome someday."

But we needed some help. Many of us were getting hurt during the marches, and hundreds of us were being arrested. The jails were full, and things were getting out of control.

Sometimes it seemed that the more we spoke out for our rights, the more some white people hated us. Some of them joined a group called the Ku Klux Klan, or the KKK for short.

The KKK burned with anger towards us. They did not want black people to have equal rights, and they did everything they could to hurt us.

In towns all over the South, the KKK beat up black people with baseball bats, pipes, and chains. A friend of mine was hurt so badly that he had to spend the rest of his life in a wheelchair. Sometimes the Klan burned crosses on our lawns. They murdered people, too.

The Klan even hanged black people by their necks from trees. This was called lynching.

I remember the night that my brother called me and said, "Martin, the KKK has bombed my house. The house is destroyed, but my family is not hurt."

"Thank God everyone is OK," I said. Over the phone, I could hear people singing "We Shall Overcome!" I was proud to hear them singing that song of hope even during such a frightening time.

The year 1963 was an important one for our movement. In June of that year, President John Kennedy really took our side in a speech on national TV. In the speech, he said that all Americans should be treated the same. I could feel that big things were about to happen.

Chapter 9

I Have a Dream

Martin Luther King, Jr. giving the famous speech
where he said, "I have a dream."

In August 1963, we took our message to Washington, D.C., in a big way. One hundred years had passed since President Abraham Lincoln had helped to free the slaves. We decided to remember the anniversary of that order by marching on Washington.

So on the 28th of August, 250,000 people of all colors marched on our nation's capital. We gathered in front of the statue of Lincoln.

On that day, I gave a speech that was seen and heard all over the country.

It was my famous "I Have a Dream" speech. I stood up in front of thousands of people and told them about my vision for the future.

I said, "I am happy to join with you today in what will go down in history as the greatest demonstration for freedom in the history of our nation."

The crowd cheered.

"I have a dream that little black children will be able to join hands with little white children as sisters and brothers!" I said.

The crowd roared with applause.

"I have a dream that my four little children will one day live in a nation where they will not be judged by the color of their skin but by the content of their character!"

Thousands of people were with me in Washington, but millions more were watching on television. They saw what I saw — an ocean of smiling faces. And on that day, a wave of hope spread across America.

But the good feelings did not last
long.

On September 15, a church in
Selma, Alabama, was bombed, and four
little black girls were killed. Two months
after that bombing, President Kennedy
was shot and killed in Dallas, Texas.
Our movement had lost a great friend.

But none of this could stop us now.
Before President Kennedy died, he had
presented a new civil rights law to the
U.S. Congress. The next year, that law
became the Civil Rights Act of 1964.

The act was passed by Congress and signed by the new president, Lyndon Johnson.

This new law gave us a lot of what we needed. It made all segregation illegal.

At last, the signs that said whites only were taken down at lunch counters, drinking fountains, bathrooms, swimming pools, schools, movie theaters — everywhere.

The new law was a great victory for black people around the country.

And this new law meant that our hard work was really starting to pay off. Little by little, we were changing America.

In that same year, when I was 35, I was given the Nobel Peace Prize. This award is given to people who work hard for peace. I was the youngest person ever to win the prize. At the awards ceremony, I told the crowd, "I still believe that we shall overcome."

Of course the Civil Rights Act didn't solve all our problems. It was a big step in the right direction, but we still had a long way to go.

Martin Luther King, Jr. holding the Nobel Peace Prize.

Some black leaders did not think that new laws and peaceful demonstrations would ever bring us equal rights. One of these leaders was a man named Malcolm X. He believed that when a white person struck a black person, the black person should strike back. He thought that black people should build their own communities and not live with white people.

I thought Malcolm X was wrong. I thought that the only way for America to live in peace was for white people and black people to love each other.

Some people agreed with Malcolm X, and some people agreed with me.

But even though I did not agree with Malcolm X, I did respect him. Sadly, he was killed in 1965.

Chapter 10

The Last Day

Martin Luther King, Jr. stands on the balcony of a hotel with other civil rights leaders on April 3, 1968. The next day, he was killed on this balcony.

The year is now 1968. I am 39 years old. It has been more than ten years since the bus boycott in Alabama.

So much has happened in the last ten years. We have marched and protested for thousands of days. We have made a lot of progress, but so much more is still needed.

I am sitting in a hotel room in Memphis, Tennessee. Tomorrow I will lead a march to help the black workers of this city.

Black people here in Memphis are not being treated fairly at work. They are being paid less than white people who have the same jobs.

Sometimes it seems like my work will never end. It seems like there will always be hatred and racism. I sometimes worry about the future of mankind. I'm afraid some of us will never understand that every person is created equal. I wonder if the people of the world will ever learn to live like sisters and brothers.

I believe that my mother was right when she said, "Some folks don't have enough love in their hearts."

In many years, when all my work is done, people will probably remember me as a fighter, but I don't feel like a fighter. I feel that all I've done is try to fill peoples' hearts with love.

And tomorrow, I will try again.

* * * * *

But Martin Luther King Jr. never got to lead that march in Memphis. At 6 o'clock in the evening, as he walked out onto the balcony of his hotel room, King was killed by a shot from a nearby building. It was April 4, 1968.

The funeral was held in Atlanta, Georgia, the city where Martin was born. Thousands and thousands of people came to express their love and thanks. Martin's father gave a speech at the funeral and said, "It was the hate in this land that took my son away from me."

Martin Luther King, Jr.'s family at his funeral in Atlanta on April 7, 1968

A few days later, Martin's wife Coretta led a march in Memphis, Tennessee. 19,000 people marched with her to honor Martin's life.

How different would the world be if Martin had lived to continue his work? We will never know. We remember Martin Luther King, Jr. as an ordinary man who became a hero. We remember him for his courage and love. And we remember him for his words.

King said, "I must confess, my friends, that the road ahead will not always be smooth. There will be rocky places. Difficult as it is, we must walk on in the days ahead with faith in the future."

Bibliography

Selected Sources

Bull, Angela, *Free At Last! The Story of Martin Luther King, Jr.* New York: DK Publishing, Inc. 2000.

King, Martin Luther, Jr. *The Autobiography of Martin Luther King, Jr.* New York: Warner Books, Inc. 1998.

Myers, Walter Dean. *I've Seen the Promised Land.* New York: Harper Collins Publishers. 2004.

Pastan, Amy. *Martin Luther King, Jr. A Photographic Story of a Life.* New York: DK Publishing, Inc. 2004.

About the Author

Eric Metzgar lives in New York City. He is a writer and a filmmaker. Eric writes short stories and poetry and he has made films about animals, about prison, and about the environment. In his free time, Eric likes to photograph people, trees, and animals, especially his two black cats, Stella and Rainer.

About the Narrator

Cedric Young was born in Chicago, Illinois. He has acted in films like, *Backdraft* and *Home Alone II* and on TV shows like *E.R.* and *Law and Order*. Cedric feels lucky to be an actor. He is also very proud to have worked for the Chicago fire department for 12 years. Cedric also enjoys playing softball and basketball, and coaching young athletes and performers.